CW00863028

ASHTON

Escaping the Island

PAUL YOUNG

Copyright © 2022 Paul Young

All rights reserved.

CONTENTS

CHAPTER ONE

It was dark and starting to feel cold and she knew she had to find somewhere warm for the night.

She had been travelling for hours and walking these streets for how long, she didn't know. She had no phone and no watch to tell the time.

The mainland had not been as welcoming as she had hoped. The few people she had seen, probably returning home from a night out, had simply ignored her.

With only a few dim street lamps to light the dark harbour-side street perhaps they had not noticed she was cradling a new-born baby wrapped in a hospital blanket under her left arm, and was clearly in need of help.

The heavy blue denim satchel slung over her right shoulder was taking its toll. The baby was fast asleep and she felt exhausted.

Behind her she could hear the gentle lapping of the water against the harbour wall and the sound of boats swaying in the moonlit marina.

The only other sound came from a pub on the other side of the road as the last customers left to head home.

She stepped slowly onto the tarmac road and made her way towards the cobbled street opposite lined with picnic benches with brightly coloured parasols, most collapsed, with just a few still raised.

Now the pub was deserted with just a dim light from the bar now remaining she could safely sit down for a much-needed rest.

Just as her foot crossed the dashed white lines marking the centre of the road, a car came hurtling around the corner, nearly knocking the all-important bag from her shoulder.

The loud noise of the car's exhaust and the calls of "Oi, Oi" from the occupants hanging out of the window almost made her lose her footing and stumble back into the path of the speeding car.

One of the passengers threw a glass bottle smashing onto the ground near her feet as the car sped off around the corner. She regained her footing and paused, briefly contemplating if it would have been easier for both of them if she had just been killed by that maniac.

Not remembering the steps at all she must have taken, she was now on the cobbled pavement scattered with tables.

A young man about her age was now standing in front of her asking if she was OK. She had not seen him come out of the pub to collapse the remaining parasols and collect the last few empty glasses.

"Are you alright miss?" he asked again in a caring, but persistent tone, insistent that he should get an answer.

She just nodded, not quite sure what to say to him.

"Come inside," he said, putting down the glasses he had dutifully collected.

"Shall I carry that?" he asked, reaching out towards the heavy, burdensome bag. She clutched it tight, like life depended on it, and shook her head vigorously.

The kind stranger immediately withdrew his hand and went back to the table to pick up the empty glasses again.

"This way," he ushered as he climbed the few stone steps to the door of the pub.

She was so tired it felt like climbing a mountain, but once inside the deserted pub, she could immediately feel the warmth of the dying fire in the huge fireplace.

He closed the door and dragged the table nearest the fire away from a cushioned bench, before throwing an extra log on the fire.

The young woman sat down.

"I'm George", he said, "and this is my mother Brenda", pointing at the lady behind the bar who she had not noticed until now.

The stout lady's presence startled her at first, but she immediately started to feel at ease seeing both had friendly faces.

"What's your name?" asked George. She hesitated for a moment before answering quietly, "Ashton".

"And your baby?"

She squeezed the baby closer and answered immediately, "Mila".

"They've been out there for hours," George informed his mother.

How did he know that, the young woman wondered to herself. She had no idea how long she had been wandering the streets of this town but had no doubt she had been walking round in circles and probably passed the pub more than once. He must have seen her while clearing glasses earlier in the evening.

"You must be exhausted," said the lady behind the bar in the same caring tone her son had spoken in.

"Get her a bowl of soup," she instructed her son, "then she can stay in room 3; it's all made up for that London couple who didn't turn up".

George and his mother left the room and she and the baby were alone again. The only sounds were the crackling of the warm fire which had sparked into life again after the kind young man had put another log on it, the gentle sound of the baby breathing, and her own heartbeat, which for the first time since she started on this epic journey seemed to have slowed.

The young man, George, returned a few minutes later with an enormous bowl of vegetable soup, still warm, with a chunk of bread on the side.

The soup was probably homemade and been kept warm on the stove all day, the bread was most likely freshly baked for lunchtime and would have been served warm too for customers arriving earlier in the day.

She dunked the bread into the thick soup and took a bite. To her this was perfect, just what she needed, and she quickly demolished the entire bowl, using the last of the bread to clean out every last drop of the delicious soup.

"I shan't have to clean that!" claimed George, who might have been standing there the whole time she ate. She had no idea.

"Let me show you to your room," he said.

The baby was still fast asleep cradled under her left arm, but she briefly panicked as she felt for the heavy bag which had been dragging on her right shoulder for so long.

It was of course right next to her on the bench.

She stood slowly and followed George to a door at the far end of the bar. He held the door open as she walked through and up the narrow staircase. Despite there being far more of these steps than the few stone steps she'd struggled to climb into the pub a short time ago, climbing these was much easier, now she had eaten.

"It's to the right," said George from somewhere below her on the stairs, "number 3".

She lifted the old-fashioned latch of the white panelled short wooden door and entered the dark room.

George was now right behind her and flicked the light switch.

In front of her was a double bed. There was a small sink, an old-fashioned wardrobe that looked too big to get up the narrow staircase and through the tiny doorway, a chair, and a small window overlooking the harbour, the curtains open.

"I'll leave you to it", whispered George from the doorway, "I'm in number 7 if you need anything, just down the hall. Mum's in the room marked private, other end of the hall". He pointed back beyond the stairway.

"Good night, Ashton," he said as he quietly closed the door, and the latch clicked.

She lay the baby girl gently down in the middle of

the bed. It was the first time she had put her down since she first picked her up so many hours ago and vowed to keep her safe.

This was the safest she had felt all day, perhaps longer than that.

Still not completely content with the simple latch on the door and no lock, and despite the good nature of her hosts, she wedged the chair against the back of the door.

She went over to the little sink in the corner of the room and cracked open the cold tap. She splashed her face with the refreshing water and cupped her hand to scoop some up to drink. She took two good swigs before looking up into the small mirror above the sink.

She could see how tired she was and briefly considered how lucky she was to have ended up here.

Then she noticed the blue denim bag strap still over her right shoulder, and immediately remembered what she was escaping from.

She looked in the mirror, over her shoulder to the tiny human being in the centre of the large bed, still fast asleep and completely oblivious to her fate.

She turned off the tap and the light and still with the heavy bag over her shoulder, climbed onto the bed and curled herself around baby Mila.

She tucked a huge soft pillow under her head and thinking how comfortable the bed was, she almost instantly fell asleep.

CHAPTER TWO

The young woman we now know as Ashton woke to the gentle glow of the morning sun shining through the small window of her room and the soft cries of a new-born baby just waking beside her. She had intentionally left the curtain open so she would be woken by the sunrise, but she had slept so well on the comfortable bed, and she had hoped Mila would still be asleep.

Quickly she grabbed the heavy denim bag still over her shoulder as she sprung out of bed. She desperately wanted to get Mila fed before she started really crying for it and drawing attention. Though still a little wary, she figured her kind hosts would not be an issue but she now realised she had no idea if there were any other guests staying in the rooms above the pub she had stumbled into the night before.

Also, she had met the kind landlady and her son last night but did Brenda have a husband, would he be as nice? And how long would it be before the people she was running from would catch up with them? Were they even actually chasing them? She had no idea but she couldn't wait here to find out. She had to get Mila away from the harbour town where they had landed on the mainland.

Luckily there was a kettle on the small bedside table that she hadn't noticed the night before.

She filled it with water from the little sink and switched it on. While it boiled she dug into the bag for a bottle, some baby milk powder and one of the hundreds of little glass injection vials that weighed down the huge bag. It was these little vials that would keep Mila alive.

She put four scoops of milk powder as per the instructions on the tub into the bottle and filled it with water from the just boiled kettle. Then she grabbed the vial, which was of course designed for injections, and wrestled with the top. It wasn't designed to come off, but she had no syringe to inject it with and she was convinced that putting it in Mila's milk would do the job.

She held the neck of the tiny vial on the edge of the bedside table and struck it with the base of the kettle shattering the glass completely. The lifesaving liquid within just disappeared into thin air and her fingers were now bleeding.

She swung around in an instant to see that Mila was still only just stirring and had not been woken suddenly by the glass-splintering crash.

Her gaze moved to the door still jammed shut by

the chair she wedged against it but nobody came.

In the distance, outside the small window she could hear a clock chiming the hour. She counted, two, three, four, five, and silence. It must be only 5am, too early for most people to be awake thankfully.

She looked down at the blood dripping from her hand. It was only a scratch, but she had destroyed one of the all-important vials, and she could not afford to do that again.

She quickly rinsed the blood from her hands in the little sink then thought again about how to get into the vials.

She grabbed another vial from the bag and this time wedged it under the front edge of the drawer in the little bedside table.

With the tiny cap wedged by the drawer she grasped the tiny bottle as hard as she could and gave a sharp tug down.

To her amazement it worked.

She poured half the liquid into the bottle, placing the vial onto the bedside table. She screwed on the teat and shook the bottle vigorously. Then she ran it under the cold tap for a few minutes to cool it.

When she thought it had probably been long enough she squirted some onto her forearm to check, just as baby Mila started to cry, a proper hungry cry.

Quickly scooping her up, Ashton held the bottle as Mila greedily drank the milk and the life-saving vial liquid. Ashton stared at the door again for what seemed like an eternity.

Had the sound of Mila's crying woken anyone? How long would it be before someone came crashing through the barricaded door? Who would it be? One of the kind strangers who had taken them both in, or one of the people they were running from?

Again, she wondered if they would actually chase them to the mainland. Were they already safe?

But she couldn't risk it and knew they had to get out of the town before the next ferry arrived. Or would they even come by ferry, there were of course plenty of smaller boats on the island, fishing boats and the like that they could also use to get here.

Luckily, she had given Mila her bottle just in time and she had stopped crying, and the door remained closed.

Ashton now stared down at Mila, who was just finishing the bottle. Safe for now at least, she thought, staring into the baby's blue eyes and just catching what she swore was a smile, while considering just how much she looked like her mother.

She couldn't concern herself with Ashton's fate

right now though, only Mila's.

Was the plan with the vials really going to work? Was half the vial enough? Too much perhaps? She didn't really know.

She knew from her time at the hospital that islanders who needed to visit the mainland were given the injection before they left.

But they would quickly return and the same injection was needed every time they left.

She had heard of a few people who had tried to leave the island, all around her own age, without the injection, against their parents' orders, and they had never been seen again. A few days later there would be a funeral, the whole island would be in mourning, and stark reminders were given to all young people never to venture off the island.

On these dark days the mainland ferry would not sail and there would be no tourists.

Ashton was not born on the island, she had visited as a child with her parents and fell in love with the beauty and quaint charm of the place.

When she had passed her first nursing exams, she moved to the island to finish her training as a midwife. The island was in desperate need of medical staff and so she was one of the very privileged few who was allowed to stay, most off-islanders having to make their way back to the mainland after their day trip.

It was shortly after moving to the island she had met a young blue-eyed girl the same age as her, who would become her best friend.

That was the girl who yesterday gave birth to a beautiful baby girl she named Mila, to whom she had vowed to keep her safe and get her off the island.

That was the real Ashton, and who knows what had become of her by now.

CHAPTER THREE

Louisa awoke in her big comfortable bedroom. Mila was awake but settled in her cot beside the double bed.

She got up and drew back the curtains and looked out over the fields.

It was months now since she left the island, and the day she first used Mila's mother's name as her own.

She thought once again about George and Brenda, as she often did in the morning, and how the two kind strangers must have felt when they found room number 3 empty that next morning.

As soon as she had fed and changed Mila, she washed out Mila's bottle, put the other half of the vial liquid into it, packed the heavy denim bag and left.

She moved the chair she had used to wedge the door shut, quietly lifted the old metal latch and crept out of the door, with baby Mila asleep once again, cradled in her left arm, the heavy denim bag once again slung over her right shoulder.

She carefully descended the narrow staircase, crept across the deserted bar, the welcoming fire from last night now completely extinguished, and after sliding the two hefty bolts open, she slipped out of the front door of the pub and away into the early morning. She didn't even turn to look back as she wandered through the quiet town streets.

Whenever she heard the occasional car approaching, she would turn to look in a shop window, making sure she kept baby Mila out of sight.

She didn't take much notice of what was in most of the windows but she did notice a really nice dress in a charity shop window and some clothes for Mila in a budget fashion store.

One window was an estate agents, with beautiful pictures of very expensive looking houses.

She remembered looking at a £1.75 million farmhouse, that looked just like the one she was in now and thinking how nice it would be for Mila, Ashton and her to live there.

How lucky had she been to find Skewes, a large stone-built farmhouse, and the elderly farmer and his wife that lived there.

Louisa and Mila's room seemed to be the only bedroom in the house with an en-suite bathroom.

As far as she could tell not even the owners had their own private bathroom, they always used the one on the hallway.

Louisa is sure this used to be a Bed and Breakfast, and she was in the family room.

She suspects this was the elderly couple's own bedroom off-season, but they had happily given it up for her and baby Mila.

After dressing herself in one of the two charity shop outfits she had hung in the wardrobe, ignoring her nurse's uniform hanging at one end, and dressing Mila in one of the many brand-new outfits neatly folded in the dresser, she gently closed the bedroom door, the blue denim bag with just a few dozen vials remaining hanging on the back of it.

Louisa didn't remember ever mentioning the gorgeous baby outfits she'd seen that morning, but every other weekend it seemed the farmer and his wife would return from their shopping trip to the nearest big town, and present baby Mila with a new outfit.

They never asked any questions about how they ended up here, they just seemed incredibly happy to have young people to look after again.

There were no pictures of children on the walls so Louisa assumed they had none of their own.

It was 7:15 so her breakfast was already on the

table as the farmer's wife always served breakfast promptly at 7am.

Three slices of bacon, two fried eggs and mushrooms, with a glass of freshly squeezed orange juice and Mila's bottle of milk sat in a bowl of hot water on the table.

It was usually two slices of bacon but it was Friday so Louisa always got the last slice from the pack.

Louisa placed Mila down in the old but well cared for playpen near the fireplace in the room the farmer's wife called the parlour.

The farmer had brought it down from the attic the day after they arrived and spent the next few days in the old hay barn sanding it and painting it until it looked as good as new.

It looked perfectly fine to Louisa when he had first brought it down from the attic and was so looking forward to putting Mila in it, but the farmer insisted it wasn't good enough.

Mila loved her playpen and the colourful toys the farmer and his wife had brought back from town for her. Louisa sat down at the table and dutifully ate all her breakfast, followed by the glass of juice last of all.

Louisa hated mushrooms but felt she could not say anything to the amazingly generous farmer's wife as she didn't want to offend her. So she always gobbled them up last and washed the horrible taste away with the juice.

"I can't stand 'shrooms either", the farmer had once whispered to her when he noticed her dislike of the ugly vegetables on her breakfast plate. He clearly didn't want to offend his wife either so neither of them ever said anything about it again.

Whenever she caught a glimpse of the old man while eating her breakfast they just gave a knowing smile and a wink.

A few moments later the farmer's wife appeared from the kitchen across the hallway where the couple would always have their breakfast.

"Lovely morning Ashton, any cereal today?" she would always ask.

With the exception of the first two days after she had arrived, when she was starving from her travels, Louisa would always say no thank you. She had given Ashton's name when she first met the couple and although she felt safe with them now, she had never found the right time to tell her story.

The elderly farmer had told of when he would be up with the sun years ago to bring the cows into the dairy for milking.

He always told the stories with fondness and a smile. The farm was a hundred acres with almost as many cows at one time, yet he seemed to have names for every one of them. When he retired, he sold all the land and his herd to a neighbouring farmer, just keeping the farmhouse, the yard and old dairy, one small field surrounded by trees and the old hay barn.

The neighbouring farmer had upgraded to robot milking machines.

"The cows love it", he had claimed, "They basically milk themselves whenever they want."

But the old farmer was not convinced, "Molly and Rose wouldn't like it," he protested. "They need to know someone cares about them."

Louisa assumed the old couple would have got their milk direct from their neighbour, from their old herd, but she was now sure that was not the case, having witnessed the familiar plastic bottles from the supermarket being brought home from their regular shopping trips.

Clearly they felt very strongly about this. Whenever he got to the bit about retiring and selling his beloved herd the farmer's heart-warming smile would always turn to a slightly sad look. But not really sad, like he knew really that he had to give it up.

Then he would glance over at Mila in her playpen, and back at Louisa and give a big smile.

It was clear the farmer and his wife were more

than happy to have guests to look after again.

Louisa took the small vial she had popped into her pocket before coming downstairs and pierced the top using the metal skewer which lay on the table for this very purpose.

Louisa had initially tried to hide the small vials and struggled trying to open the tiny bottles in various ways. She had no idea what her hosts might think they were and didn't want to risk being kicked out or reported to the police, or worse.

But one morning the skewer was on the breakfast table. Louisa had no idea what for.

After clearing her breakfast things, the farmer's wife slid it across the table towards Louisa and simply said, "I think this will help."

The skewer was always there every morning after that and Louisa figured the farmer's wife sterilised it along with Mila's bottle as it was hot to the touch when Louisa arrived for breakfast on time.

Still no questions were asked and nothing more was said.

She poured some of the contents of the vial into Mila's bottle, secured the top and gave it a good hard shake. The vial now two thirds full she placed back on the table and she would remember to take back to her room for another day.

Mila now looked at her surrogate mother from the

playpen, eager to drink her formula.

Louisa was very conscious she was not Mila's real mother, but she was the only one she had really known and she had sworn to take care of her.

Mila guzzled down her breakfast and Louisa gave a sigh of relief. It was only recently, maybe a couple of weeks ago that Mila had refused her bottle and Louisa swore she looked off colour.

Was she starting to get ill from being off the island for too long? Had the half vial of the normally injected clear fluid in her milk been enough?

Thankfully the kind farmer's wife sensing Louisa's desperation at not being able to get Mila to take her formula had offered to help.

Reluctantly, Louisa handed the now crying baby over and the bottle of still warm milk.

Within seconds Mila started drinking and within no time had finished the lot.

As baby Mila finished the last drops of milk from her bottle, Louisa wondered again what she would have to do when the vials ran out.

She had taken every one she could cram into the denim bag as she hurried out of the island hospital, but they were nearly all gone already. She had lost countless doses trying to open the fiddly little glass bottles while searching for somewhere safe for the two of them to stay, and before the arrival of the skewer.

How grateful she was for the skewer. She had not lost a drop since, and although she had reduced the dosage down to a third of a vial every day, she knew they would run out soon, perhaps a month.

Mila needed the life-saving doses to stay off the island, but Louisa had no idea what the little vials actually contained. The tiny labels only had a QR code batch number on them and an expiry date, which luckily was far enough in the future, but no help in identifying the contents.

"You OK dear?" enquired the farmer's wife.

"Oh yes, just daydreaming," Louisa quickly replied.

"Well, you have a good day at work, the little one's safe with us, think we might go on the swans again today," she said cheerfully, smiling at Mila and offering her hands out to take her.

She was referring to the swan-shaped pedalos on the Coronation Boating Lake on the outskirts of town which Mila absolutely loved.

It was £10 for twenty minutes but the farmer and his wife seemed to know everyone in town and they never paid.

Even when there was a big queue of tourists, the couple would be ushered to the front into the best available swan pedalo, to the looks of absolute disgust from the family waiting impatiently at the front of the queue.

The silver-haired gentleman running the pedalos swiftly took their £10 and pointed them at the very grotty looking frog pedalo at the edge of the lake. Nobody wanted the frog pedalo.

Even baby Mila would give a hint of a baby frown whenever they walked past it.

One of the young lads helping the farmer and his wife, and Mila into the gorgeous swan pedalo offers them three lifejackets.

The farmer helps his wife to wrap Mila in the oversized lifejacket but both shrug off the idea of wearing one themselves.

The mother of the two impatient boys now sat in the cold wet puddle at the bottom of the frog pedalo turns to the silver-haired gentleman.

"Life jackets?" she enquires sternly.

"Not deep!" he replies in a gruff South West accent as he throws the wet mooring rope in her lap and gives the pedalo a hard shove with his boot, rocking it violently.

"He nearly pushed us in," screeched one of the impertinent children.

The silver-haired gentleman shrugged his shoulders as he turned his back on them, and then gave a cheerful wave towards Mila and her surrogate grandparents.

"Hi Mila," he waved.

They never went more than half way across the lake and were rarely back within 20 minutes, due to neither of the old couple having particularly flexible knees any longer. Louisa knew however that Mila would enjoy her day and she felt that they were both safe in the care of the very lovely old couple.

With the recommendation of the farmer, Louisa had got a job waiting tables at the café down the road which proudly claimed to be the most southerly on the mainland.

During the summer it was usually local boys and girls back home from university that got this job, but it was the off-season now and the gentleman that ran the cafe was near retirement himself.

He didn't want to give up just yet, but the farmer had convinced him he could use some help in the off-season.

It seemed everybody knew everybody around here and at first Louisa had felt very nervous about being an outsider, but it had become clear very quickly that with the farmer and his wife's recommendation she was accepted by everyone as one of the locals.

In fact, she felt more at home here than she had anywhere else in her life.

All the locals seemed to know who she and Mila were, of sorts. They all thought her name was Ashton of course and they must have assumed they were related to the old couple somehow. The exact details of their fictitious relationship never came up in conversation so Louisa had no idea how everyone thought they were related.

To be safe, she was always careful not to say anything to anyone that might conflict with anything the old couple might have said before.

It had been a busy day at the café for off-season. The sun had shone all day and the view was spectacular as always.

This was good as it helped Louisa to keep her mind off worrying what she and Mila would have to do next.

But she was on the bus home now. It still felt strange to think of the remote farmhouse as home, but it definitely did feel like home.

The café owner had paid her cash from the till as always. With most people paying by card or with their phones these days she wasn't sure exactly where all the cash in the till came from, but she was paid every day without fail.

Today she had got £5 extra. It was clearly a good day, and she figured the café owner genuinely appreciated the help that had been so politely forced upon him by the farmer a few weeks ago. Though he never said that.

It was an energetic walk up the hill to the small village where she would catch the bus.

The village green was surrounded by tourist shops and cafés. Most of the cars that had been parked on the green during the day had now gone and the shopkeepers were putting away the beach balls and buckets and spades, and closing up shop for the night.

One of them waved at Louisa from across the road and she waved back as an annoying young boy dragged his equally annoying mother into the shop to buy some silly toy.

In this off the beaten track little village you couldn't turn away customers at closing time, especially off-season.

Louisa was sure the boy should have been at school today, but it wasn't unusual to see families taking holiday in term time these days, even in England.

The bus pulled up opposite the long-abandoned pub at the crossroads and Louisa stepped off onto the grass verge. There was no official bus stop here.

"See you tomorrow Ashton," said the friendly bus driver as the doors closed behind her and he drove off.

She couldn't remember if she'd ever heard the

farmer or his wife introduce her to the bus driver, or if someone else must have said something, but she was sure she had never introduced herself.

It was only a few minutes' walk down the narrow country lane shaded by tall trees from the crossroads to the farmyard gate.

She crossed the farmyard and entered the front door of the farmhouse into the hallway.

The farmer and his wife were sat in the parlour, the TV on quietly. She was knitting, obviously something for Mila. She held it up but Louisa had no idea what it was going to be.

"Shh," she whispered, "little one's asleep in your room. She's had a very busy day."

"Me too, I'm gonna go straight up."

Louisa had been given dinner at the café before her shift ended.

The farmer laid back in his favourite armchair, worn out and covered in duct tape, and had his feet up on a small wooden stool.

"Just going to catch the headlines," he probably said to his wife as the local news started on the TV.

But no sooner had the news reader announced the first report, the old man was snoring with his eyes tight shut.

Louisa used to sit up with them to watch the local

news, checking for any reports of a missing baby snatched by a reckless trainee midwife.

But the report never came and she had now given up checking. She didn't even look at the local weekly paper anymore. When she first got her job she used to wait until the old couple had gone to bed before slipping a £20 note under the place mat that was already laid out for breakfast in the morning.

But come the next evening, it was always still there.

Louisa thought at first that perhaps the old lady had missed it and tried to make it more obvious she had left the money out intentionally for the generous couple.

Eventually she figured they just didn't want to take it, and so now she had given up leaving the money out.

Instead, she headed on up the stairs to her room where Mila was sleeping soundly in her cot as promised, another new toy alongside her.

This one was a cuddly green frog which made Louisa chuckle as she remembered the boating lake, the annoying boys and the woman with the wet rope in her lap, that time she had gone with them. She wondered what fun Mila and the old couple had had today while she was working.

She had a warm shower, washed and brushed her

blond hair which seemed to be growing quickly after she had hacked it so short in their early days on the run.

She kissed Mila on the forehead and climbed into her bed, quickly falling asleep.

CHAPTER FOUR

For weeks now Louisa had been contemplating how she was going to get hold of more vials for Mila.

She still had no idea what they contained or how to find out. As far as she knew they were only made on the island.

She had considered telling the whole story to the old couple who Mila and her now lived with or going to a local hospital, but she had never heard of this strange condition unique to those born on the little island before and figured neither had anyone else on the mainland.

They would want to keep Mila for endless tests and she didn't want that for her.

She also thought briefly about taking Mila back to the island, but quickly dismissed the idea. It was too dangerous for her and it was against her mother's wishes.

Besides, if they were looking out for them returning to the island it would be far easier to sneak in alone.

So that was the plan, to go alone, to grab as many vials as she could from the little hospital on the hill and get back to Mila as quickly as possible.

She knew Mila would be safe at the farm but couldn't bring herself to say anything to the farmer or his wife.

The plan had started the night before when she took a pair of sharp scissors from the farmhouse kitchen up to bed with her.

Mila was fast asleep in her cot as usual after a typically exhausting day with her surrogate grandparents.

Louisa wondered what fun they had had today, feeling incredibly lucky that Mila had these two wonderful people in her life to care for her, while she hacked her blond hair really short once again with the sharp kitchen scissors. A hairdresser she was not but that didn't matter. She wasn't getting ready for a date after all.

She was going to save Mila's life, she desperately hoped.

Next, she carefully applied the dark brown hair dye to every strand of hair.

She counted down the seconds on the old-fashioned alarm clock on the bedside table. The thirty minutes required for the hair dye to fix was frustratingly long as Louisa had nothing to do but sit and wait, considering all the things that could possibly go wrong tomorrow.

Would she even get out of the front door? She knew she would have to leave incredibly early to catch the tourist ferry in the morning, but now realised she had no idea what time the farmer or his wife woke up in the mornings. They were always up before her.

The second her thirty minutes were up she jumped in the shower and rinsed the dye out of her hair, watching it run down her legs and into the drain at her feet.

She towel-dried her hair in no time, there were advantages to short hair it seemed and stared back at herself in the large oval mirror above the dressing table.

It'll do, she thought to herself, it will have to do.

CHAPTER FIVE

Sleepily she opened one eye to peek at the old alarm clock. It was just after 4am, far earlier than she needed to be up, but far better to get up now than to oversleep. She had to do this today, Mila's life depended on it.

She got herself dressed, putting on the baseball cap with a Lizard on it and the backpack she had bought last week from one of the little shops on the village green.

The girl, or perhaps even boy, looking back at her in the mirror now looked like a typical tourist, exactly as she'd hoped.

She took with her only enough money for the journey to the island, plus some snacks and drinks, leaving the rest of the money she'd earned working at the café on the dressing table, along with the three remaining vials and a note.

She gently kissed Mila on the forehead being very careful not to wake her and left the farmhouse, hoping it would not be for the last time.

"Going the wrong way aren't you, Ashton?" asked the friendly bus driver as she stepped onto the northbound bus she had flagged down at the crossroads opposite the derelict pub.

"Day off," she lied.

It was Saturday and she should indeed have been going to work later in the morning.

As she sat down half way along the empty bus she felt bad about letting down the café owner, but she had to go on a weekend when there would be lots of tourists and the ferry didn't sail on Sunday, her normal day off.

Of course she hadn't told anyone of her plans and she just wouldn't turn up today.

The bus terminates at the railway station where Louisa and the three other passengers picked up along the way get off.

The friendly bus driver said goodbye but Louisa either didn't hear him or just ignored him as she focussed on her mission.

She bought a return ticket from one of the automated ticket machines and bought a bottle of water, two packets of crisps and a stale looking pre-packed croissant from the little coffee shop on the platform.

The local buses were timed to connect with the main line trains so she didn't have long to wait.

She waited until everybody who wanted to had got off the train, then stepped off the quiet platform and on to the train, sitting down in the first available seat, and placing her empty backpack on the seat near the window.

As the train pulled out of the station, she started to eat the dry croissant and had a swig of the refreshing bottled water, looking out of the large window from her rear-facing seat at where she had just come from.

The long train curved around the huge stone-built viaduct that dwarfed the streets below and as it headed west into the countryside it picked up speed and everything outside became a blur.

The train soon reached the end of the line and Louisa hurried off the train and along the platform to the automatic ticket barriers. She popped her outbound ticket in the slot and stepped through the barrier as it opened for her. She moved at a brisk pace along the harbour-side towards the ferry docked alongside the harbour arm.

It was much easier in the daylight and without the weight of a new-born baby and the heavy denim bag over her shoulder. This time she had come better prepared with the sturdy tourist-style backpack.

But she still needed to buy her ticket and board the ferry which was due to depart soon for the little island.

It seemed like only yesterday her and baby Mila had escaped and now she was going back there.

She joined the back of the queue outside the little ticket office that used to be a weighbridge. The locals here still took social distancing very seriously with the tourists, though they quickly seemed to forget when the tourists had all left for the day.

So only two customers were allowed in the little ticket office at a time, everyone else had to queue outside, even in the pouring rain.

Where Louisa now stood, George and Brenda's pub was right behind her. She turned and glanced at the front door, not yet open for the day's customers, but quickly turned back to the front of the queue.

She was feeling incredibly nervous and worried she would miss the boat but now more tourists had joined the queue behind her so she figured it wouldn't leave port without them.

Everyone was paying with contactless cards or their phones so the queue moved quickly and Louisa was soon standing in front of one of the two ticket desks. Louisa would of course be paying for her ticket in cash.

"One student day return," she requested.

"Got any ID love?" enquired the middle-aged woman wearing a crisp white shirt with the island ferry's logo on it from behind the makeshift plastic divider.

Louisa had realised her mistake as soon as the words had come out of her mouth.

She had brought enough money with her for an adult ticket, remembering at the last minute she couldn't use her island residents' discount but why had she said student?

She was still a student in theory but she'd ditched her real identity months ago when she left the island and of course couldn't use it even if she hadn't gotten rid of her student ID card.

Oh yes, let's just tell them we're coming shall we.

She quickly reacted and started fumbling in the pockets of her jeans and the little side pockets of the backpack.

"I think I must have left it in my dorm this morning," figuring this sounded better than, "Oh sorry, I meant adult."

She was just about to hand over the extra cash when the woman behind the counter slid the return student ticket through the small opening at the bottom of the divider and smiled.

"You have a nice trip dear," she beamed, and turned her gaze to the next customer waiting patiently at the doorway as she beckoned them forward.

Louisa eyed a small group of tourists about her age just about to join the queue at the entrance to the long harbour arm to board the ferry. She sprinted across the road to catch up with them.

If she was travelling in a group, she was less likely to be spotted she thought.

"Hi!" she chimed as she caught up with the group just picking up their own backpacks, three girls and two boys she now realised.

"Going for the day?" she asked, "Mind if I tag along?"

"Yes," replied the shorter brunette girl, "You going on your own?"

"My roomie pulled out last minute, doing something else with her boyfriend".

"We're Exeter," the stranger replied, referring to their university.

"Plymouth," Louisa responded, hoping that was a safe choice and that none of her new travel companions knew anyone from Plymouth.

With her head down Louisa handed her boarding card to the man at the bottom of the gangplank. He marked it with a fat marker pen and handed it back to her.

Louisa followed the Exeter girls up the gangplank and onto the ferry. The two boys followed a minute or two later after one of the men on the harbour arm searched both their backpacks, checking, Louisa assumed, for alcohol or drugs. But they found nothing, which was a relief, as if they had then they might have called the girls back off the boat.

Louisa could hear the two boys whispering to each other as they climbed the gangplank behind her, but she couldn't work out what they were saying.

"Ryan likes you," one of the other girls said, "He saw you queueing for your ticket."

"There's seats over here," the third girl exclaimed, grabbing Louisa's hand and dragging her towards the back of the boat.

There were just four empty seats between a family with a toddler and two older ladies travelling together. The four girls sat down in the empty seats leaving the boys to find their own somewhere else on the ship.

Louisa was sat next to the two older ladies. The nearest one introduced herself as Joyce and her travelling partner was Mary.

They had been best friends since school and since both their husbands had now passed, they had spent the last two and a half years travelling the country together, visiting every National Trust garden that didn't have too many steps.

When their husbands were alive, Joyce's holidays

were always to little steam railways, frequently in North Wales, and Mary's were always to see old buses and trams.

The one time the four of them went away together they stayed in an old railway carriage for three nights.

It was very uncomfortable and they never went away together again. Now Joyce and Mary were visiting all the places, they wanted to see.

It was clear Joyce was the talker in their relationship and Louisa was grateful of the distraction from the monotony of the two and a half hour ferry trip.

Now and again the girl sat to her left who had dragged her to her seat interjected and asked Louisa about her days at university.

Luckily Louisa had a few tales to tell from her days at uni over a year ago but she had to be careful with details as she hadn't actually attended Plymouth like she had claimed.

With about half an hour left to go, everyone else's attention turned to the rocky island rising out of the sea off the starboard side of the boat.

Starboard is the proper name for the right-hand side of a ship she had learnt on one of many previous sailings on this very boat.

Joyce's husband had convinced her that the right-hand side of a ship was called port.

Louisa overheard Joyce recalling this fact to Mary while also recalling having a glass of the fortified wine of the same name in her hand at the time.

So whether Joyce's husband was wrong, or Joyce simply remembered the facts incorrectly as a result of being rather sozzled at the time remained a mystery so far.

Though Louisa was convinced she herself had remembered correctly, and catching sight of a bottle of the aforementioned drink in Joyce's oversized handbag finally convinced her it was the latter.

Mary was no saint either, smuggling two plastic glasses and a corkscrew in her own large bag.

Neither of the old ladies had realised the cheap bottle of supermarket own-brand fortified wine had a screw top.

While everyone else admired the view, Louisa thought back to her arrival on the island to continue her midwifery training, all those months ago.

CHAPTER SIX

Two men of the Island Guard stopped a young man descending the gangplank in front of her as soon as he stepped on to the harbour arm built of solid granite blocks, and escorted him into a small unsigned room at the end of the little white terminal building.

He looked a few years older than Louisa and she assumed he had been spotted by someone on the ferry trying to smuggle alcohol or drugs onto the little island.

Any sort of drugs and excessive alcohol consumption were very much frowned upon by the island residents, and they much preferred the tourists to spend their money buying their drinks on the island.

Louisa had spotted an official looking, middle-aged man but not in any uniform she recognised, walking around the ferry during the lengthy crossing, seemingly looking at everyone and their bags as he went.

He had paid particular attention to the young

man sat opposite her and after that she hadn't seen him again on the crossing.

She now deduced the official-looking man must have been an agent for the Island Guard, and was sure now that he must have reported the young man now being escorted from the quayside for potentially bringing contraband onto the island.

She was sure the young man would be released once his duffle bag had been searched and any contraband confiscated.

She had heard about the island's strict policy on alcohol, but was still surprised at the effectiveness of the measures taken to enforce it.

She suspected though that the confiscated liquor would end up on sale behind the bar of the harbour-side pub. That must help with profits she mused, knowing how much the tiny island economy relied on tourism.

The mainland police rarely visited the island as crime rates were so low, in fact by the time Louisa hurriedly left the island about a year later she was not aware of one crime being reported.

The tight knit island community sort of policed the island themselves through the Island Guard.

A small band of middle-aged men volunteered for this official-sounding but very much unsanctioned role. They wore a uniform, a navy-blue shirt with the island logo on the breast pocket and a number of gold stripes on the sleeve just below the shoulder denoting the Guardsman's rank.

On the very rare days that a PC from the mainland would bother to make the five-hour return trip, the Guard would assume the roles of friendly guides to disembarking tourists, with an acknowledging nod to the guest constable or perhaps even a formal salute.

But every other day the men of the guard would be seen checking everyone off the boat, making sure no tourists missed their return sailing, and ticking off the resident youths for every minor indiscretion from dropping litter to cycling on the well-manicured lawn of the memorial square.

The Island Guard used the old courthouse as their headquarters, which was now the community hall, but it seemed appropriate.

They had a little office with room for just two small desks at the back of the wooden panelled hall, behind the small raised platform where the magistrate appointed by the king used to preside over legal matters of the remote community.

The office used to be the magistrate's chambers and the little raised platform was now used as a stage to call out bingo numbers at the weekly event hosted by the island W.I. or by members of the seven-strong, *Societe Photographique des*

Island, when presenting their latest efforts with an antiquated slide projector perched on a precarious shelf at the other end of the little courtroom.

The photographic club thought their name made them sound more authentic, but they had only formed a couple of decades ago, their translation was poor, and there was no historic evidence the French had ever occupied this tiny outpost of England.

Still, occasionally one of them would take a pretty good photo.

Every month they voted the best photos to be printed, mounted and displayed in the wooden framed display case on the front of the stone-built building.

And the occasional tourist, with either poor taste or poor eyesight would snap them up.

Any money they made after the costs of printing and framing would be donated to the community hall committee towards the upkeep of the historic building.

Another door on the opposite side of the platform from the Guard office led to a narrow winding stone staircase to a small basement.

It was cold and damp and contained just two tiny cells with rusty cast iron gates.

In return for donations for the old building's

upkeep, the Guard members offered tours of the building to eager day visitors.

They would tell tales of some of the more gruesome cases allegedly tried in the old courthouse, but even the most gullible were unlikely to believe some of the torturous punishments the Guard claimed were carried out.

The more able visitors on the tours were taken two at a time down the narrow winding staircase by candle light to see the tiny cells.

The candle light was purely for effect as they'd had electric lights fitted a few years ago at great expense to the hall committee, after one of the older members of the photographic club slipped on the bottom step.

You'd think after that health and safety would have put a stop to taking tourists down the treacherous well-worn steps by candle light, but not here.

One of the cells was now used to store cleaning materials, equipment belonging to the photographic club, the W.I. bingo machine and some anonymous wooden crates. Confiscated liquor perhaps?

The other cell had a varnished wooden bench, a bucket in the corner and a large metal chain with a very modern looking padlock was dangling from the slightly open iron gate.

"And this is where we put the delinquent youth," announced the slightly overbearing tour guide, to chuckles of laughter from the amused tourists.

A tour of the cells was a regular trip for the island's school children and they took the seemingly idle threat far more seriously.

The tour was one of the first things Louisa did when she arrived on the island, keen to learn about its history and culture, but she never believed any of the island's young people had ever actually been forced to spend the night down here. That would just be cruel.

She even attended one of the photographic club meets and the first W.I. bingo night after she arrived.

At both meetings she was offered a free cup of tea and a biscuit by a gentleman named Derek, according to the scrawled sticker on his knitted jumper.

The jumper, Louisa assumed, was supposed to depict the beautiful island, but it was hard to tell.

Derek explained the jumper was knitted by his wife of 43 years, who was a member of the W.I. committee and explained his presence at both meetings.

Derek half-filled a china tea cup with a picture of a very young Queen Elizabeth II on it with steaming hot water from a large boiler sitting on a rickety old trestle table at the side of the hall.

He dunked a fresh tea bag into and straight out of the boiling water, hardly changing the colour of it at all and threw it straight in the bin under the table. He then poured enough milk into the cup to make the tea completely cold again, whispering, "Say when," just as it reached the brim.

Derek placed the cup on a mismatched saucer, followed by a stale homemade biscuit, and offered it forwards.

In the other hand he thrust another saucer loaded with small change in front of Louisa's path as she turned to leave the table, clearly expecting a donation in return, for the free, hot, drink.

She quickly realised all the attendees at these events were well over twice her age, if not three times over, and neither the island art scene of the photographic club nor the stereotypical knitting and baking of the W.I. when her grandmother was still a regular attendee were the kind of social life she was hoping for right now.

Perhaps when I'm ninety she thought to herself, if I'm still here by then.

She stepped out of the W.I. meeting onto the quiet street opposite the sweeping bay. Perhaps island life was not all she had dreamed it would be as a little girl and she had made a big mistake moving here from her home back in the south-east of England.

Just as she was about to turn up the hill to head back to the house where she was staying, she caught sight of a small group of friends on the golden sandy beach the other side of the low sea wall opposite the former courthouse.

Louisa crossed the quiet road, stepped over the low wall and onto the soft sand.

She approached the two girls sat on the sand to introduce herself.

The girl in the cream blouse and the powder blue knee-length skirt turned to face Louisa as she fought her way through the shifting sand towards them. Her blue eyes matched the colour of her skirt and her long blond hair matched the warm tones of the sandy beach.

"You must be the new girl," she said, "I'm Ashton and this is Madison. That's my boyfriend Stuart over there and Maddy's fella Smithy," she continued in full flow pointing at the two lads larking around in the clear blue sea in front of them.

Louisa had no idea which of the boys was which and assumed Smithy was a nickname.

"You're a nurse, right?" the inquisitive girl continued without taking a breath.

"Trainee midwife," Louisa corrected her, "my name's Louisa".

"Pleased to meet you I'm sure," Ashton responded.

The other girl, Madison or Maddy, didn't say much and the boys stayed in the water for ages, but Ashton could talk and she had plenty to say, but nothing of any real significance.

Louisa had finally found a friend on the island and they quickly became best friends. It soon felt like she had known Ashton since they were little kids.

Ashton would tell Louisa everything. They never saw that much of Madison or the boys after that evening.

Stuart was supposed to be Ashton's boyfriend but they didn't seem to ever spend much time together, which Louisa thought rather odd, but she never said anything.

Ashton and Louisa would sometimes sit on the hillside below the old garrison walls above the harbour to watch the ferry come in.

They would rate the boys they saw coming off the boat out of eleven.

Eleven was supposed to be reserved for the very best-looking young men but in reality they were too far away to make any accurate assessments and they were probably way too generous with their elevens.

One day they had witnessed one young man being escorted into the little room by the Island Guard and spent all day trying to guess what he might have been smuggling.

Tourists only get four hours on the island before they have to return to the mainland on the ferry. The girls sat on the hill all day waiting for the apprehended young man to reappear from the little building but he never did.

They were just about convinced they must have simply missed him and were about to head home when about half an hour before boarding time for the return sailing, two men of the Island Guard went into the little room and escorted the man back out again and straight on to the ferry.

They took him down to the lower deck then just one of the Guard men came back ashore.

When the ship came to sail, all the man had seen of the island was the harbour arm and the inside of the little room.

Two and a half hours each way and four hours in a little room. He must have been really peeved. What could he have possibly done wrong to warrant his incarceration?

The girls went home sunburnt that day having spent far too long on the hill.

Their favourite place to sit though was the bench by the lighthouse on the opposite headland above the beach where they had first met.

It was here on this very bench that Ashton had

told Louisa the news, "I'm pregnant," clutching her belly as the words fell out of her mouth.

Louisa was a trainee midwife and although Ashton didn't show yet, she'd noticed the signs days ago and had been itching to congratulate her best friend as soon as she told her. She didn't want to spoil the announcement knowing that Ashton would tell her when she was ready. And maybe she'd want to tell her parents first or Stuart.

But Louisa could tell from the tremble in her voice and the look on her face that she was scared.

All first-time mums are nervous but Ashton was frightened, petrified even.

"They're going to kill me," she exclaimed, "or put me in those terrible cells and take my baby away."

"Who?" challenged Louisa.

"The Guard of course."

"They don't really do that," Louisa replied in a calming voice, putting her arm around Ashton's shoulders.

"They do!" her terrified friend insisted lurching away from her disbelieving best friend.

Louisa slid along the bench closer to her friend again, putting her arm once more around Ashton's trembling shoulders.

"OK, OK," she said, trying her best to calm Ashton

down, "I'm sure Stuart's mum will help."

Stuart's mum was none other than Mrs. Hilary Wainwright-Harris, the most respected lady on the island. The local young people called her Lady H but never to her face.

Lady H was chair of the Community Hall Committee, chair of the W.I. and treasurer of the Fundraising Committee for the little hospital where Louisa worked. Surely if anyone could help it would be her.

"But she is the worst," screamed Ashton, "no way!"

"But surely if it's her own grandchild."

"It's not," Ashton interrupted, "Stuart and I never."

Louisa was slightly taken aback by this shocking statement.

Ashton and Stuart had been together for years, she knew from Ashton's stories how strict the islanders were about being married before having children, but she almost couldn't believe that they never had.

Ashton went on to tell a story she had never even alluded to before.

A few days before meeting Louisa for the first time she had been watching the ferry passengers disembark from the hillside above the harbour and spotted a group of students.

In the middle of the group was a tall slim hunk of a young man, a definite eleven, maybe even a twelve.

Louisa and Ashton had never given anyone a twelve.

Ashton rushed down the steep path to the main street nearly twisting her ankle on the way, in the hope she might bump into the boy.

As luck would have it, he bumped into her, completely by chance as she bent down in the middle of the crowded street to tie her shoelace which had come undone in her mad sprint down the hill.

He nearly went head over heels straight over her but recovered his balance quickly and offered his hand to help the pretty young woman up from the ground.

As she looked straight up at him from the bumpy, hard, cobbled street, she was initially blinded by the sun directly behind him and couldn't see his kind face.

Once to her feet she could tell immediately it was the twelve she'd been chasing down here in the hope of catching a closer look at.

On closer inspection he perhaps wasn't the hunk she'd first imagined from afar, but he was charming. Far more the gentleman than Stuart Wainwright-Harris these days.

By now his university chums had abandoned him, having seen their mate had already found himself an exciting tourist attraction.

"I'm Matt," he said with a huge smile.

"Ashton," she giggled in response, "can I show you the sights?"

"Pretty good view right here I think."

He quickly backtracked, "Sorry that was really cheesy. What I meant was I would love a tour of the island. I've always wanted to come."

"I'm doing photography," he informed her, pulling his expensive mobile phone from his back pocket, "Landscapes."

None of the islanders had mobile phones as there was no signal, but tourists would of course bring them to take photos and to pay for their food, drink and souvenirs.

Ashton took Matt to the top of the island first and they worked their way back down.

There were huge fields growing bright yellow daffodils, which provided the island with its only other source of income besides tourism.

All the photos Matt took though were either selfies of the two of them or photos of just Ashton.

Was he really studying photography, Ashton thought, as he seemed to have got his landscapes confused with his portraits, or did he just say this as an excuse to get his camera phone out? She didn't care though.

She was the centre of his attention the whole time and she loved it.

After a couple of hours, they reached the secluded secret garden that only the locals knew about.

They hid themselves away in a corner of the pretty garden, enjoying each other's company until it was time to return to the ferry.

Ashton wasn't looking for any kind of relationship from the relative stranger, she knew he would return home and she'd never see him again, but she also never expected to get pregnant her first time.

This probably explained why she hadn't seen as much of Stuart recently.

Did Ashton tell him about Matt, Louisa wondered, or had they just drifted apart before she even saw Matt that day?

Two weeks before her due date, sat on their bench near the lighthouse, Ashton explained her plan to a reluctant Louisa.

The plan was madness, Louisa argued, but the heavily pregnant Ashton made her swear to get her baby off the island and protect him or her from the islanders, and to never bring them back here.

Louisa listed every hole in the plan she could think of.

What if they were caught before they got off the island? Couldn't Ashton come too? Of course she couldn't, the strange Island Curse as the islanders called it, meant she couldn't possibly escape the island herself.

Louisa still couldn't believe the stories Ashton had told her about the mystery illness, but her friend was adamant.

She could not leave the island herself but her baby might be OK if Louisa could get hold of enough of the injection vials from the little hospital.

Perhaps the baby would not even develop the killer condition if she left the island as soon as she was born.

CHAPTER SEVEN

It was a difficult labour but Louisa helped her friend deliver a beautiful baby.

"It's a girl," she announced, placing the little bundle onto Ashton's chest.

"Her name's Mila, and you have to get her off this island now!" Ashton insisted. The ferry would leave soon.

Louisa grabbed the blue denim bag she had helped Ashton prepare with a bottle, milk powder and nappies, and rushed out of the little maternity room down the short corridor to the store room where they kept the little vials.

There were no fancy swipe cards here like a large mainland hospital, just a simple four digit keypad lock which she had seen the other nurses open hundreds of times.

She scooped as many of the tiny vials as she could into the bag and raced back to her friend and baby Mila.

She pleaded one last time with her friend to

reconsider, but she insisted Louisa had to run.

How she got out of the little hospital in the middle of the afternoon, through the town and onto the ferry she still had no idea.

She immediately went down to the little room on the lower deck where nobody usually wanted to sit. There were no windows and the constant vibration of the engines, but Louisa had gotten used to it on her occasional visits to the mainland and the vibration of the engine was probably helping baby Mila to sleep.

Now she was back on this very ship and the gangplank had just been wheeled up to the open deck ready for today's tourists to disembark.

CHAPTER EIGHT

It was 7:45 and Ashton had still not come down for her breakfast and the farmer's wife was starting to worry.

The mysterious girl they had taken in with her little baby girl Mila just a few months ago was rarely on time when her cooked breakfast was put on the table promptly at 7am every day, but she was never this late.

Then she could hear baby Mila start crying upstairs in the family room. She immediately went to investigate knocking on the bedroom door at the end of the upstairs hallway. She slowly opened the door part way peering into the room.

She could see baby Mila crying in her cot and worriedly called out "Ashton!"

There was no reply, so the opened the door wide. The bed was empty and there was nobody else in the room.

She picked Mila up out of her cot and the baby instantly started to calm.

She tentatively opened the en-suite bathroom door calling Ashton's name again, but it was also empty.

Where could she be? She would not have abandoned the little baby girl that she took so much care of, surely?

As she turned back to head out of the room she noticed the hand written note on the dressing table, alongside a stack of bank notes and three of the tiny vials that went into Mila's morning milk every day.

"Trevor," she called out urgently, but not too loudly so as not to startle young Mila, "Trevor".

The farmer came running up the stairs as fast as he could and stood in the doorway stooped over trying to catch his breath.

Even just a few years ago when he still milked his beloved cows every morning he felt as fit as a man half his age, but that had all gone now.

He glanced up at his wife cradling the baby in one arm with the scrappy note in the other.

"She's gone!" the shocked woman announced.

She read the note aloud to her husband.

"I've gone to get more medicine for Mila.

Please look after her while I'm gone.

She needs 1/3 of a vial in her milk at breakfast.

I've left all my money in case I don't make it back.

If I don't, and the medicine runs out please take her to hospital.

Love

Ashton."

Obviously things were far worse than they had ever imagined. The farmer's wife showed her husband the three little vials.

"Those will only last a week," he exclaimed, "we're not waiting. Get her fed and dressed, we'll take her to Doc Trevelyan now."

Ashton was clearly scared of the authorities and didn't want to take Mila for any of her jabs or check-ups that a new-born should have.

But the old couple trusted the local doctor who they of course knew as well as anyone in the surrounding villages.

While his wife tended to the baby, the farmer went across the yard to the old hay barn to collect his nine month old shiny electric car.

He had used some of the money from the sale of the farm to buy the top of the range off road EV and to fit solar panels on the barn roof.

He could drive all over the county for free and they even made money from the excess electricity they fed back into the grid.

He had put far more panels on the barn roof than the salesman had recommended, but it was a sound investment, especially with the soaring prices of electricity, petrol and heating oil.

He pulled up by the front gate to the house and was just checking Mila's car seat was securely in place as his wife brought her out to the car.

He didn't really need to check as the well-padded seat never left the car and was always securely fastened, but he religiously always checked before Ashton or his wife put baby Mila in it.

"We're going for a little ride in Molly," the old farmer gently whispered to Mila, having named the fancy car after his favourite member of their former dairy herd.

They hurtled towards the local GP surgery at breakneck speeds, the old farmer handling every bend of the narrow twisting country lane perfectly. Normally his wife would be reprimanding him for his reckless driving, but not today.

They soon arrived at the little surgery and notified the young receptionist of their arrival.

A few moments later, Doctor Trevelyan appeared at his consulting room door seeing out his previous patient.

He was about to call the next woman in line, when he caught sight of the old couple and the little baby.

"Do you mind?" he said to the lady as she was about to get up from her waiting room chair, beckoning forward his old friends without waiting for a response.

She shook her head with an approving smile.

"What can I do for you, old friends?" he asked as the couple sat down in front of the GP's large old wooden desk.

The couple explained the vials handing over one of them and their concern for the missing young woman and the little baby, passing him the scribbled note too.

He checked baby Mila over, his cold stethoscope on her chest making her giggle.

"Seems perfectly healthy to me," he confidently pronounced, "but of course you can't always tell," came the authoritative warning.

"And you've no idea what this medication is?" he enquired.

Both shook their heads as Mila giggled again playing with the fluffy green frog toy they had brought with them.

"Well I'll get this one tested by the hospital lab but it may take a few days!"

"Can't it be done any quicker doc?" challenged the farmer.

"I'll get it done urgently but cultures do take time, there's no way to rush it I'm afraid. It just depends what is actually in here, it might come back sooner."

"What should we do now?" asked the farmer's wife.

"Keep giving her the same dose I guess until we know more, until then just wait, sorry. I'll call you as soon as I hear anything."

The farmer drove sedately back to the farm, and the three of them waited as instructed, for either a call from Doctor Trevelyan or for Ashton to walk through the front door.

CHAPTER NINE

Louisa slipped easily past the Island Guard in her excellent disguise in the middle of her small band of travelling companions.

Once through the stone archway at the landward end of the harbour arm and onto the cobbled main street, the group paused to consult their tourist maps and work out where they would go first.

Louisa knew exactly where she was headed though and just kept walking without even a goodbye.

She marched straight up the hill out of the miniature town at a pace, towards the little terrace of whitewashed cottages where Ashton lived.

As she approached along the gravel track towards the western headland she hesitated, looking for any signs that Ashton's parents might be at home.

Then she turned left onto a narrow path that went behind the terrace and on towards the cliffs.

She stared intently at the windows at the back of the house looking for any signs of movement while crouching behind a large prickly thicket. She grabbed a handful of small pebbles from the path and started throwing them one by one at the window of Ashton's bedroom, with no idea if her best friend would be in.

Her aim was dreadful and not one of the tiny stones hit its target. She stood up from behind the thicket and launched the remaining gravel in her hand at the back of the little house.

They clattered on the window pane startling the girl inside lying on her bed, listening to her favourite music with her head in a book.

She immediately leapt to her feet and peered through the glass. At the sight of her very best friend cowering behind a thicket at the end of her garden the biggest smile appeared on her face, and she hastily tore off down the stairs.

Ashton opened the back door to see Louisa now half way up the garden. The green mesh fence had long since collapsed and on this quiet and safe little island her father had never bothered to fix it.

But her face fell when she realised Louisa was alone. She rushed out of the door and flung both arms around her best friend.

"Where's Mila?" she worriedly enquired.

"She's safe, really safe, and she's really well, but the vials have nearly run out. I came to get more, but

I had to see if you were alright first."

The pair went into the little house and Louisa told her friend all about the farm, her job at the café and the pedalos.

Ashton then explained that after hearing she had gone to the hospital to have her baby, Lady H went straight there.

She was absolutely furious that the baby was gone and ordered the Guard to find her, but she was too late.

Ashton heard the two short blasts of the departing ferry's horn signalling it had left the harbour, and she raised the corner of her mouth into a slight smile.

"You stupid little tart," the extremely angry woman yelled at her, "You've killed that baby and deprived that lovely couple of the child they deserved."

The smile vanished.

She was referring to a middle-aged couple who had lived on the island their whole lives, married at sixteen but couldn't have children of their own.

Lady H had promised Ashton's unborn child to them at the start of her second trimester.

Ashton did not like the couple at all though and was convinced that getting her baby off the island was the only option.

She had not previously told Louisa about the forced adoption as she knew Louisa would try to convince her to go through with it.

That heated debate came now.

The two soon calmed down though, both realising the argument was now completely pointless.

It felt like they'd only been together again for five minutes but they'd actually been talking for nearly two hours.

Louisa still had to get the life-saving vials she came for from the island hospital and get back on the ferry unnoticed before it departed to head back to the mainland.

Now she had fully recovered from the ordeal of giving birth Ashton wanted to come too.

If they stole enough vials, and syringes too then she would be able to leave and to see her baby girl again, even if it was just for a few days. She would happily face the consequences on her return.

It was risky but Louisa couldn't really argue this one.

Ashton quickly grabbed a bag and threw some clothes in, they left the little house and Ashton slammed the door behind her.

She didn't leave a note, completely disillusioned with her parents who were less than supportive after finding out she was pregnant. When they found out it wasn't Stuart's they simply ignored her.

On the orders of Lady H she was effectively under house arrest and never ventured beyond the front gate anymore, but her parents never spoke to her.

CHAPTER TEN

Louisa suggested it would be safer if Ashton waited outside the little hospital while she went in for the vials and syringes.

Luckily they had not changed the code to open the little room labelled *Drug Store*, and there were hundreds of the little vials on the shelf.

She scooped them all into the backpack and zipped it shut.

Next she opened a small cabinet and took out a dozen small syringes, placing them in the rucksack's largest front pocket.

She lifted the fully laden bag onto her shoulders and carefully opened the door.

She peered into the corridor to ensure her exit was clear and calmly walked past the unmanned reception desk out into the hospital car park.

There on the little patch of grass next to the flagpole flying the island's very own flag was Ashton; flanked by two burly members of the Island Guard.

"Hello again miss," said one of them sternly, "fancy seeing you back here. I'll take that thank you."

Louisa reluctantly handed over the backpack of life-saving vials.

"Wait there," he said, as he took the bag back into the hospital. He dropped it onto the reception desk and walked back to his colleague and the two girls.

"This way," he ushered, leading the way down the road towards the town.

Both girls were heartbroken at their failure.

Louisa wondered what would happen to them now. Ashton knew exactly what was coming.

All the tourists had now left this end of town eager to pick up some last minute souvenirs from the shops nearest the harbour before they had to board their ferry home.

Other men of the Island Guard made sure none of them would miss their sailing.

The students Louisa arrived with didn't look for her after she abandoned them when they arrived.

They all assumed she would find her own way.

Louisa now wished she had asked them to look out for her instead of just deserting them.

The four of them walked into the old courthouse and one of the two Guardsmen entered the little office behind the little raised platform.

He returned seconds later with a key.

He walked over to the little door on the other side of the room and switched on the stairway lights.

He led the way down as the other Guardsman ushered the girls silently towards the narrow staircase.

The first man ushered them into the empty cell, closing the heavy iron gate behind them and securing the hefty chain with the padlock. The two men returned back up the narrow steps and closed the door again at the top.

The girls waited a moment for it to go dark, but the men at least left the dim electric lights on.

"They won't keep us in here overnight though will they," said Louisa optimistically.

Ashton gave a look that said otherwise and then burst into tears.

CHAPTER ELEVEN

The telephone rang in the hallway of Skewes farmhouse and the farmer leapt from his favourite armchair to answer it while his wife continued to play with Mila on the parlour floor.

The familiar voice of Doctor Trevelyan spoke on the other end.

"Are you sure?" the farmer queried.

"One hundred percent," replied the doctor.

"Thanks doc," the farmer said as he put down the phone, immediately picking it up again and dialling 999.

"Police," he said firmly.

"What on earth is going on?" his wife asked him now standing right beside him with baby Mila in her arms.

"We have to find her," he said.

"I need to report a missing person," he said into the phone, "and it's urgent."

CHAPTER TWELVE

It took about 48 hours, but good old fashioned police work had helped Detective Inspector Russell of the Devon and Cornwall police to conclude the girl everyone knew as Ashton was heading for the Island.

The farmer's wife had a good picture of the four of them; the farmer, his wife, the girl and baby Mila, on her mobile phone.

It was taken by the silver-haired gentleman who ran the pedalos while they all sat in Mila's favourite swan, one Sunday morning. She couldn't work out how to do it herself but one of the tech guys at the police station copied the photo and ran off dozens of prints.

The local bus driver said he'd dropped Ashton off at the station the day she disappeared and the station CCTV showed the time she bought her ticket.

Knowing the exact time, the railway company were able to look up what ticket she had bought and also confirmed she had used her outbound ticket in the automatic barrier at the station at the western end of the main line.

She had purchased a day return so she clearly intended to come back that day but her return ticket was never scanned at the automatic barrier and logs showed there were no faults with the barrier that day.

CCTV at the terminus confirmed she left the station that morning heading towards the harbour and there was no sign of anyone jumping the gates later in the day.

The railway CCTV operator was ordered to review every tape thoroughly from that morning until today for any sign of the young woman, while the police started door to door enquiries.

DI Russell figured the island was a strong possibility for her destination from here though he still had no idea why.

But the staff in the ferry ticket office did not recognise the young blond woman from the photograph the police showed them.

Just as the experienced DI stepped back out of the little ticket office, unsure of his next move, George descended the steps of his mother's pub opposite.

The DI walked across to the young man collecting glasses and showed him the photo.

He immediately recognised the girl and the baby, though she had clearly grown since he saw them.

He was very happy to see they were both well and smiling in the family photo.

He assumed the old couple in the photo he didn't recognise must have been Ashton's parents or grandparents or some other relations.

With no idea why the police were searching for her or what trouble she might be in, he initially said nothing.

Sensing hesitation and his gut telling him the young man might know something, DI Russell revealed, "She's not in any trouble but it is very important we find this young lady. She's abandoned her baby girl and she might be in danger."

"That's Ashton and Mila," replied George.

He proceeded to tell the DI of the night they had arrived at the pub from the island. He knew that's where they had come from as the hospital blanket Mila was wrapped in had the name of the island's little hospital embroidered along the edge.

He was also sure he had seen her again two days ago standing in the queue for ferry tickets.

She had changed her hair but he recognised her cute frame and the way she walked.

He didn't reveal this much detail to the DI though. He was just adamant it was her.

He had tried to get down to speak to her but by the time he'd got dressed and downstairs she was long gone, half way along the harbour arm towards the ferry and she never saw him waving at her from the road. Without a ticket he couldn't get on to the arm while the ferry was docked.

DI Russell didn't need convincing though, he was already on his mobile to headquarters.

"I need two DS's and the force helicopter here in fifteen minutes, and the rest of the team on that island as soon as possible!"

A police constable who drew the short straw was a very rare sight on the island, so even without mobile phones, news of a Detective Inspector and two Detective Sergeants landing by helicopter from the mainland spread round the island in no time at all.

They commandeered a taxi from the tiny helipad on the hill and ordered the driver to take them into town.

They intended to split up and start handing out the photo to everyone they saw, hoping to recruit some of the local Island Guard members to do door to door enquiries.

But as soon as they stepped out of the taxi they were stopped by a young man just dumping his bicycle at the side of the road.

"You know this young woman?" enquired DI Russell.

"The Guard have them," the young man replied, "in the cells below the courthouse."

"Cells!" exclaimed the DI.

"You two, over here!" he shouted at his two sergeants just as they were heading off towards the town. They hurried back and the three officers and the young man burst into the community hall.

Two Guardsmen appeared from the little office to see what the noise was.

The Guard were used to making their own rules and not taking orders from outsiders, but they instantly recognised the authority bestowed by the metal badge thrust in front of them by the mainland police officer standing in the middle of the hall flanked by two other plain clothes officers.

"Go with him," the DI ordered as one of the Guardsmen returned to the little office, wanting to make sure he wasn't going to make a run for it out of any back door he didn't yet know about.

The two returned soon enough, this time with a key.

DI Russell followed the Guardsman down the narrow staircase.

There was a strong smell of urine and despite the young man's tip off he was still shocked to see two young women locked up in the tiny cell with nothing but a wooden bench, a single bottle of water, and the bucket which he now realised was the source of the smell.

Without prompting, the Guardsman unlocked the chain and heaved open the rusty gate.

As they stepped through the narrow doorway at the top of the stairs Ashton was surprised to see Stuart standing in the middle of the room. It was the first time she had seen him since before she gave birth to baby Mila.

"Arrest those two for kidnap and false imprisonment for starters," DI Russell instructed the DS's.

Stuart turned to the DI and just said "You'll be wanting to speak to my mother next."

DI Russell raised an eyebrow.

"Actually I'd like to hear your stories first," he said, looking directly at Ashton and Louisa.

The girls relayed their incredible story to the DI.

When they got to the bit about the curse, DI Russell stopped them mid-sentence.

"It's a myth," he proclaimed, "There's no mystery illness or curse!"

"Those vials you've been giving her baby," he continued, addressing Louisa, "contain nothing but saline."

Saline was nothing more than sterile salt water,

something that was used as a placebo in double-blind drugs trials.

"Your baby," he followed on, now looking at Ashton, "has never had anything more than slightly salty baby milk in her bottle and she is perfectly fine back on the mainland".

Louisa was shocked but relieved at this revelation.

Ashton couldn't believe it. Had she been lied to all these years?

"But what about the others?" Ashton insistently queried.

"Others, what others?" asked the now completely shocked DI.

Ashton and Louisa retold the stories about young islanders who had tried to leave and never been seen again, and the secretive funerals.

Despite how far-fetched the girls' story was, the experienced DI was inclined to believe them; that something at least had happened to these people over the years.

By now the Devon and Cornwall police helicopter had made a second trip to the island and three uniformed officers now stood silently at the back of the hall listening intensely to the girls' bizarre statement while awaiting their orders.

DI Russell stood up and addressed the three PCs.

"You two, get me Lady what's-her-face; *his* mother, here now."

"You, escort these two young ladies back to the mainland on the helicopter."

Ashton looked nervous at the prospect of leaving the island.

"Don't worry," the DI reassured her, "we'll get a doctor to check you out when you land."

"Sort that out will you," he instructed one of the Detective Sergeants, who immediately got on the radio to HQ to make the request.

"This investigation is going to take months," he remarked, "and I don't even want to think about the paperwork"

CHAPTER
THIRTEEN

He was right too.

A small army of officers and a Home Office forensics team would come over on the ferry, like you see on the telly with their white coveralls, elasticated blue overshoes and popup gazebos.

They exhumed all the graves where the alleged curse victims were buried in the little island cemetery.

But every wooden coffin they prised open was empty apart from a few large rocks to weigh them down. No bodies.

The number of arrests escalated very quickly from this point, starting with Lady H, her fellow committee members at the community hall, the W.I. and the hospital fundraising community.

The island hospital doctor, head nurse and the undertaker were also charged with various offences, and even the florist.

The police even questioned the parish priest but she'd only been on the island a few years and as the phantom funerals had started long before this they were satisfied that she knew nothing and genuinely believed she was committing dead bodies to the ground.

An appeal featured on the national TV news and it would indeed take many months for all the missing islanders to be located.

They were all still alive, living all over the mainland, some of the older ones with young families of their own. One was even living on a Spanish island in the Mediterranean.

When asked why they never returned to the island or tried to contact their families, some said they simply couldn't bear to return to their oppressive homeland.

Some claimed they had tried to phone home but found their parent's numbers disconnected. They assumed their parents had intentionally changed their numbers to prevent them getting in touch.

The landlines were all managed by BT remotely by computer but they hired a local caretaker to look after the little exchange on the top of the island, a former GPO engineer who had long since retired.

That was none other than Derek.

He had no idea how the modern digital exchange

computers worked and didn't have the access codes anyway, but he still had his leather GPO tool belt and was more than capable of physically swapping the wires over that entered the building. So that was another arrest for DI Russell and his team.

A few had tried to return but had been apprehended by the Island Guard as soon as they stepped off the ferry, convinced that their parents wanted nothing more to do with them and strongly encouraged to return to the mainland without even venturing into the town.

Some parents knew of the island-wide scam of course and were in on the whole thing, but many had no idea, genuinely believing their loved ones had perished due to the dreadful Island Curse.

There were some incredibly emotional reunions as a result.

The story of the curse had been around over a hundred years but it was Lady H who had first suggested making the curse real as a way to ensure the island's young people wouldn't want to leave. If they didn't leave then their parents wouldn't sell their houses to wealthy mainlanders looking for second homes, that she convinced everyone would destroy island life as they knew it.

The idea was of course absurd but everyone always listened to Lady H.

She also revived the old Island Guard to police the

island and enforce her elaborate plan.

For her part in the whole horrible affair Lady H would spend the rest of her days in a mainland prison and would never see her beloved island again.

CHAPTER FOURTEEN

It was only twenty minutes after taking off from the island's emergency helipad that the police helicopter landed on the mainland.

As promised a doctor met them off the helicopter and after a complete check-up gave Ashton a clean bill of health.

The two girls were shown into a conference room at the police station.

Sat at the large oval table in the centre of the room were the farmer and his wife with baby Mila.

They immediately stood and held out baby Mila towards Louisa.

Louisa looked at her best friend, who stepped forward to take the baby girl.

The old couple looked bewildered but seeing Louisa's approving smile the farmer's wife gently handed Mila over to the young woman.

Mila smiled as if she recognised her mother as Ashton embraced her tightly.

"This is Mila's real mother, Ashton, my real name is Louisa," the young woman revealed.

The old couple took only a few seconds to process this new information.

"Very pleased to meet you Ashton," the farmer said, "you have a very beautiful baby girl."

"Louisa, you had us worried sick," the farmer's wife added, "You should have told us."

Louisa filled in the gaps in the story that the old couple hadn't got from the police or the news, while Ashton spent some long overdue time with her baby.

Eventually, Louisa turned to Ashton and said to her, "We need to find somewhere to stay."

"You and Mila already have a home," said the farmer's wife before turning to her husband.

"And you of course Ashton are welcome to live with us too," he added.

Ashton looked at Louisa. She had listened intently to her detailed description of the farmhouse during their imprisonment and was excited at the thought of seeing it for real.

"But you have to let us pay rent," Louisa insisted.

The farmer and his wife initially rejected the offer but reluctantly compromised on £10 each per week for the two girls to include breakfast, but would accept nothing for baby Mila.

"Bacon, eggs and mushrooms," the farmer's wife told Ashton.

"Oh thank you, but neither of us like mushrooms," she politely informed the old lady.

"Actually neither do I," the farmer sheepishly admitted to his wife.

"Grilled tomatoes then," she replied with an amused smile on her face.

The couple of course spent all the girls' rent money on Mila.

EPILOGUE

It was Mila's second birthday and they finally felt safe enough to return to the little island of her birth. Just for a day trip though.

A couple of months ago Ashton had finally reconciled her differences with her parents.

After Lady H had gone and the truth came out they had realised how foolish they had been and were desperate to make peace with their only daughter.

They had visited the mainland a couple of times to see Ashton and Louisa and to meet their baby granddaughter, and it was their idea for them to visit the island.

The brave trio, the farmer and his wife, and George sat together on the ferry as it made its slow journey across the flat sea on this beautiful sunny day.

The farmer, his wife, and even George, despite living his whole life in the pub opposite the ferry terminal had never visited the island before.

The group of six looked just like a normal family of tourists as they stepped off the gangplank onto the harbour arm, the farmer and George both looking a little green despite the calmness of the crossing.

The only thing setting them apart from the others disembarking was everyone else had their mobile phones out already snapping pictures of the harbour arm and the little white terminal building.

They were met not by the men of the Island Guard, who had been completely disbanded, but by Ashton's parents, Madison and Smithy. Madison was showing a discernible bump but no sign of a ring on her finger.

Stuart would no doubt have been there to meet them, but he had left the island a few months ago. He briefly visited the farmhouse to say hello, to meet Mila, and to tell the girls he was going to university and wanted to join the police as a detective.

The ferry was much busier than Louisa ever remembered it being, as a recent TV documentary titled *Escaping the Island* had fuelled interest in the place.

An enterprising group of young islanders had partnered with the ferry company, some of the little businesses on the island and even Brenda's mainland pub to offer a complete package tour based on the story.

Those wearing a purple wristband were met off the ferry by one of the team of young tour guides and taken first to see the old garrison, then across the bay past the little bench by the lighthouse to the top of the island.

On the way back down they saw the little hospital and got a tour of the old courthouse and the tiny cells. They didn't use candles anymore though.

The courthouse was no longer a scheduled school visit, but of course all the children previously terrified of the basement cells now wanted to visit.

Next they would visit the little pub on the island harbour-side and on presentation of their wristband be offered a tasting of one of the island's own gin liqueurs.

Under 18's were offered a glass of freshly pressed apple juice from the little orchard on the island.

Before departing the tour guide would hand out gift vouchers to be used in any of the souvenir shops in the main street.

They might put this towards a little trinket to remind them of their visit or perhaps a bottle of island gin.

On their return to the mainland they would be encouraged to visit Brenda's pub where a warming bowl of vegetable soup would always be on the menu.

The little island's economy had never been stronger.

Otherwise island life seemed little unchanged, it was still an incredibly tight knit and proud community.

The most visible change was the disappearance of the Island Guard of course.

Their little office at the back of the old courthouse was now used by the duty constable of the Devon and Cornwall police.

A PC from the mainland would be sent over to do a three month stint at a time. Far from being the short straw it was a highly desirable beat.

With a low crime rate, your own cottage rent free and no boss on the island, there was never any shortage of volunteers for the role.

There was also the *hotline* as the officers would call it. The duty PC on the island had the authority to call out the force helicopter if they ever needed it.

Anywhere else you would need an Inspector or above to call in the helicopter.

No PC had ever needed to of course, but they all loved boasting of the fact that they could if they needed it, to their colleagues back on the mainland.

Ashton and Louisa both hesitated at the front door of the courthouse community hall before nervously stepping inside.

In front of them stood in a huge arc were dozens of familiar friendly faces from the island and DI Russell and the two Detective Sergeants who had investigated Louisa's disappearance.

Between them and the crowd were three trestle tables laden with all manner of party food and in the centre a huge pink iced cake topped with two sparkling candles.

"Happy birthday Mila," Ashton's mother said aloud.

"Make a wish," she said to Ashton softly.